This Walker book belongs to:

_____

_____

Goldilocks and the Three Buffalo

Goldilocks and the Three Snakes

Goldilocks and the Three Robots

...ocks and the ...ee Pigeons

Goldilocks and the Three Elk

Goldilocks and the Three Salmon

G...

Goldilocks and the Three Opera Singers

Goldilocks and the Three Moose

Goldilocks and the Three Falcons

...the ...s

Goldilocks and the Three Cats

Goldilocks and the Three Mastodons

Goldilocks Three ...

...locks and the ...ee Bicycles

Goldilocks and the Three Deer

Goldilocks and the Three Foxes

G...

...the ...ges

Goldilocks and the Three Squirrels

Goldilocks and the Three Mice

Goldilocks Three Oa...

...locks and the ...Woodpeckers

Goldilocks and the Three Orthodontists

Goldilocks and the Three Hippos

G...

...the ...s

Goldilocks and the Three Wolves

Goldilocks and the Three Witches

Goldilocks Three Z...

...ocks and the ...ee Eagles

Goldilocks and the Three Accountants

Goldilocks and the Three Alligators

G...

...the ...ds

Goldilocks and the Three Pirates

Goldilocks and the Three Clams

Goldilocks Three C...

...locks and the ...ree Bulls

Goldilocks and the Three Eels

Goldilocks and the Three Jumbo Shrimp

G...

Goldilocks and the Three Puppies

Goldilocks and the Three Naked Mole Rats

Goldilocks and the Three Elephants

Goldilocks and the Cavemen

Goldilocks and the Three Whales

Goldilocks and the Three Giraffes

Gold... Th...

Goldilocks and the Three Mosquitoes

Goldilocks and the Three Lions

Goldilocks and the Three Moles

...he

Goldilocks and the Three Terrible Monsters

Goldilocks and the Three Apes

Goldilocks ar... Three Prin...

...ks and the ...e Geese

Goldilocks and the Three Giants

Goldilocks and the Three Chickens

Gold... Th...

...he ...s.

Goldilocks and the Three Penguins

Goldilocks and the Three Cyclopes

Goldilocks a... Three Me...

...ks and the Bunnies

Goldilocks and the Three Dogs

Goldilocks and the Three Germans

Gol... T...

...he

Goldilocks and the Three Goldfish

Goldilocks and the Three Pumas

Goldilocks an... Three Tige...

...s and the Nutrias

Goldilocks and the Three Rocket Scientists

Goldilocks and the Three Ants

Gold... Th...

...he

Goldilocks and the Three Meerkats

Goldilocks and the Three Goats

Goldilocks an... Three Cow...

...ks and the Big Feet

Goldilocks and the Three Baboons

Goldilocks and the Three Wild Boars

Gold... T...

GOLDILOCKS

and the

THREE DINOSAURS

As Retold by

MO WILLEMS

WALKER BOOKS
AND SUBSIDIARIES

LONDON · BOSTON · SYDNEY · AUCKLAND

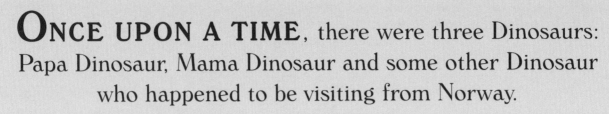

ONCE UPON A TIME, there were three Dinosaurs: Papa Dinosaur, Mama Dinosaur and some other Dinosaur who happened to be visiting from Norway.

One day, for no particular reason, the three Dinosaurs
made up their beds, positioned their chairs just so
and cooked three bowls of delicious chocolate
pudding at varying temperatures.

"OH BOY!" said Papa Dinosaur in his loud, booming voice.
"IT IS FINALLY TIME TO LEAVE AND GO TO
THE … uhhh … SOME PLACE ELSE!"

"YES!" continued Mama Dinosaur. "I HOPE NO INNOCENT LITTLE SUCCULENT CHILD HAPPENS BY OUR UNLOCKED HOME WHILE WE ARE … uhhh … SOME PLACE ELSE!"

Then the other Dinosaur made a loud noise that
sounded like a big, evil laugh but was probably
just a polite Norwegian expression.

The three Dinosaurs went Someplace Else and were definitely *not* hiding in the woods waiting for an unsuspecting child to come by.

Sure enough, five minutes later a poorly supervised little girl named Goldilocks came traipsing along.

Just then the forest boomed with what could
have been a Dinosaur yelling "GOTCHA!", but
I'm pretty sure was just the wind.

The loud noise was immediately followed by
another loud noise that sounded kind of like,
"BE PATIENT, PAPA DINOSAUR!
THE TRAP IS NOT YET SPRUNG!"

But that could have been a
rock falling. Or a squirrel.

GETTING
CLOSER!

Either way, Goldilocks was not the type of little
girl who listened to anyone or anything.

For example, Goldilocks never listened to warnings about
the dangers of barging into strange, enormous houses.

So as soon as Goldilocks came across a strange, enormous house, she barged right in.

Inside, Goldilocks immediately
smelled the three bowls of
delicious chocolate pudding.

"Mmmmm!" said Goldilocks.
"That chocolate pudding smells
delicious. If only I could get all the
way up to the top of that counter!"

Then Goldilocks noticed a very tall ladder
that just happened to be there and
certainly wasn't left on purpose.

Goldilocks climbed up the ladder
and found herself face-to-face
with three gigantic bowls
of chocolate pudding.

The first bowl of chocolate pudding was too hot,
but Goldilocks ate it all anyway because,
hey, it's chocolate pudding, right?

The second bowl of chocolate pudding was too cold,
but who cares about temperature when you've got
a big bowl of chocolate pudding?

Not her.

The third bowl of chocolate pudding was *just right*, but Goldilocks was on such a roll by now, she hardly noticed.

Soon Goldilocks was stuffed like one of
those delicious chocolate-filled-little-girl-bonbons
(which, by the way, are totally *not* the favourite
things in the whole world for hungry Dinosaurs).

Tired and groggy, Goldilocks noticed three chairs
in the living room. So she climbed down the
ladder and walked out of the kitchen.

The first chair was too tall.

The second chair was too tall.

But the *third* chair —

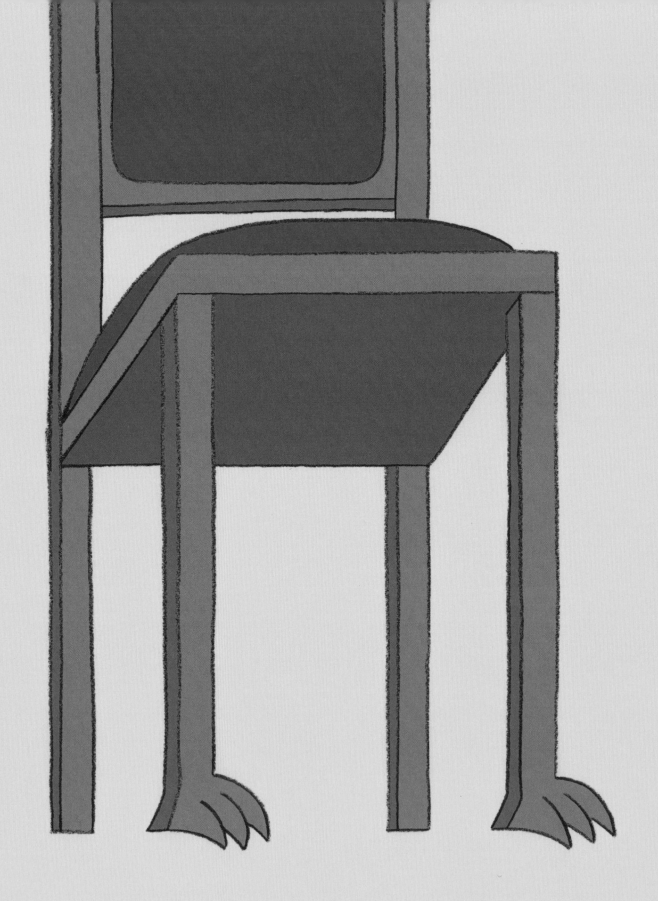

WAS TOO TALL.
Goldilocks wasn't going to climb that high just to sit
in some chair, so she trekked over to the bedroom.

When she got there, Goldilocks noticed
that the beds were also gigantically big.
"What is going on around here!?" groaned
the exhausted girl. "The bears that
live here must be nuts!"

Just then the room filled with a loud, booming noise that was either a passing truck or a Dinosaur gloating,
"A FEW MORE MINUTES AND SHE'LL BE ASLEEP! DELICIOUS CHOCOLATE-FILLED-LITTLE-GIRL-BONBONS ARE YUMMIER WHEN THEY'RE RESTED!"

Even a little girl who never listens to
anyone or anything had to hear *that*.

Goldilocks took a minute to stop and think, which was longer than she was used to stopping and thinking.

"Hey…" she told herself. "This isn't some bear's house. This is some DINOSAUR'S house!"

Say what you like about Goldilocks,
but she was no fool. As quickly as she could,
she ran to the back door and *got out of there!*

Just then a loud plane flew by, which sounded pretty much like
a trio of Dinosaurs yelling "NOW!" or "CHARGE!" or the
Norwegian expression for "CHEWY-BONBON-TIME!"

Suddenly – and completely coincidentally – the three
Dinosaurs rushed through the front door.

But they were too late.

Goldilocks was gone, and all that was left in the house were three disappointed Dinosaurs.

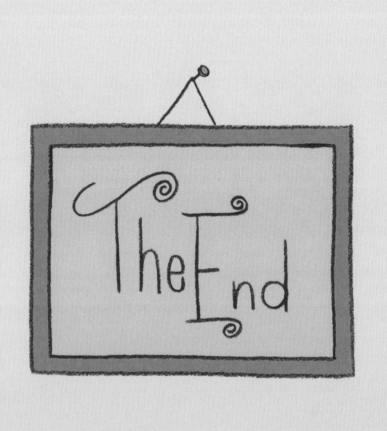
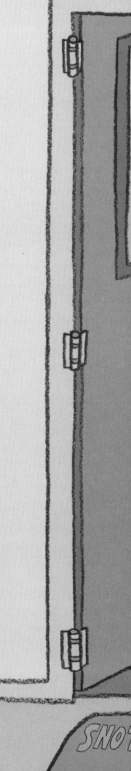

And the moral is:

If you ever find yourself
in the wrong story, leave.

And the moral for Dinosaurs is:

LOCK THE BACK DOOR!

Goldilocks and the Three Musketeers

Goldilocks and the Three Free Men

Goldilocks and the Three Xylophones

Goldilocks and the Three Poodles

Goldilocks and the Three Dudes

Goldilocks and the Three Red Herring

Go

Goldilocks and the Three Wall Street Types

Goldilocks and the Three Crows

Goldilocks and the Three Owls

the

Goldilocks and the Three Bus Drivers

Goldilocks and the Three Termites

Goldilocks Three H

ocks and the ee Worms

Goldilocks and the Three Drummers

Goldilocks and the Three Wise Men

Go T

the es

Goldilocks and the Three Condors

Goldilocks and the Three Rats

Goldilocks Three Major

Dedicated to Lee and Diane, dinosaurs

First published in Great Britain 2013 by Walker Books Ltd, 87 Vauxhall Walk, London SE11 5HJ

This edition published 2014 ❖ 2 4 6 8 10 9 7 5 3 1 ❖ © 2012 Mo Willems

First published in the United States 2012 by Balzer + Bray, an imprint of HarperCollins Publishers, LLC
British publication rights arranged with Wernick & Pratt Agency, LLC
The right of Mo Willems to be identified as author/illustrator of this work has been asserted by him
in accordance with the Copyright, Designs and Patents Act 1988

This book has been typeset in Windsor Light ❖ Printed in China

ocks and the ree Squid

the

Goldilocks Three Glass

British Library Cataloguing in Publication Data:
a catalogue record for this book is available from the British Library

ISBN 978-1-4063-5532-1 ❖ www.walker.co.uk ❖ www.mowillems.com

ocks and the ee Gerbils

G

the ls

Goldilocks and the Three Foot-Long Hoagies

Goldilocks and the Three Prairie Dogs

Goldilocks Three-Pie

ocks and the ee Bedbugs

Goldilocks and the Three Frogs

Goldilocks and the Three Deer

G

Goldilocks and the Three Snails ~~(crossed out)~~

Goldilocks and the Three Underwear Salesmen

Goldilocks and the Three Ibex ~~(crossed out)~~

...ks and the Stooges ~~(crossed out)~~

Goldilocks and the Three Roosters ~~(crossed out)~~

Goldilocks and the Three Lynx ~~(crossed out)~~

Gold... Th...

Goldilocks and the Three Robot Dancers ~~(crossed out)~~

Goldilocks and the Three Hamsters ~~(crossed out)~~

Goldilocks and the Three Motorcycles ~~(crossed out)~~

...he

Goldilocks and the Three Bears *(circled)*

Goldilocks and the Three Pizzas ~~(crossed out)~~

Goldilocks a... Three An...

...ks and the Meatballs ~~(crossed out)~~

Goldilocks and the Three Weasels ~~(crossed out)~~

Goldilocks and the Three Gondolas ~~(crossed out)~~

Gol... T...

...he ...rks

Goldilocks and the Three Pythons ~~(crossed out)~~

Goldilocks and the Three-for-One Special ~~(crossed out)~~

Goldilocks a... Three M...

...ks and the ...ile Island ~~(crossed out)~~

Goldilocks and the Three Camels ~~(crossed out)~~

Goldilocks and the Three Ostriches ~~(crossed out)~~

Gol... T...

...he ...ilk

Goldilocks and the Three Crawfish ~~(crossed out)~~

Goldilocks and the Three Snowmen ~~(crossed out)~~

Goldilocks a... Three Fren... ~~(crossed out)~~

...s and the Turkeys ~~(crossed out)~~

Goldilocks and the Three Dinosaurs ~~(crossed out)~~

Goldilocks and the Three Peas ~~(crossed out)~~

Gold... Th...

...e ...d

Goldilocks and the Three Dragons ~~(crossed out)~~

Goldilocks and the Three Peacocks ~~(crossed out)~~

Goldilocks an... Three Do... ~~(crossed out)~~

...s and the ...e Cows ~~(crossed out)~~

Goldilocks and the Three Llamas ~~(crossed out)~~

Goldilocks and the Three Elves ~~(crossed out)~~

Gol... T...

Mo Willems is the author of the Caldecott Honor-winning books *Don't Let the Pigeon Drive the Bus!*, *Knuffle Bunny* and *Knuffle Bunny Too* as well as the Theodor Seuss Geisel Medal-winning Elephant and Piggie books. An acclaimed animator and television script-writer, he has won six Emmy awards for his writing on *Sesame Street* and is also the creator of *Sheep in the Big City*. Mo lives with his family in Massachusetts, USA.

Other books by Mo Willems:

ISBN 978-1-84428-513-6

ISBN 978-1-84428-545-7

ISBN 978-1-4063-0812-9

ISBN 978-1-4063-1550-9

ISBN 978-1-4063-4009-9

ISBN 978-1-4063-0158-8

ISBN 978-1-4063-1215-7

ISBN 978-1-4063-4731-9

ISBN 978-1-4063-1229-4

ISBN 978-1-4063-2137-1

ISBN 978-1-84428-059-9

ISBN 978-1-4063-1382-6

ISBN 978-1-4063-3649-8

Available from all good booksellers

www.walker.co.uk